IN FOCUS...

CRETACEOUS DINOSAURS

Dougal Dixon

Quarto Library

Quarto is the authority on a wide range of topics.

Quarto educates, entertains and enriches the lives of our readers—enthusiasts and lovers of hands-on living.

www.quartoknows.com

This library edition published in 2020
by Quarto Library,
an imprint of The Quarto Group.
26391 Crown Valley Parkway,
Suite 220
Mission Viejo, CA 92691, USA
T: +1 949 380 7510
F: +1 949 380 7575
www.QuartoKnows.com

Distributed in the United States and Canada by
Lerner Publisher Services
241 First Avenue North
Minneapolis, MN 55401 U.S.A.
www.lernerbooks.com

A CIP record for this book is available from the Library of Congress.

ISBN: 978 0 7112 4810 6

Manufactured in Guangdong, China CC042020

9 8 7 6 5 4 3 2 1

FSC www.fsc.org MIX Paper from responsible sources FSC® C008047

CONTENTS

Words in **bold** are explained in the Glossary on page 31.

CRETACEOUS EARTH

Dinosaurs dominated the world during the Cretaceous period, which lasted from 145 to 66 million years ago. The Earth was warm, and a huge range of plants and animals thrived on the planet.

DINO DATA

Some scientists think that biting insects such as mosquitoes spread disease among the dinosaurs.

A modern world

During the Cretaceous period, Earth became more like it is today. The modern **continents** and oceans began to form as the land broke into smaller pieces. It grew colder at the North and South Poles and warmer near the **Equator**.

Some of the most amazing Cretaceous **fossils** have been found in the deserts of Mongolia.

Plant life

The first flowering plants began to grow in the Cretaceous period. This caused new forms of insect to develop. Some types of trees that survive today also emerged, including oak trees and maple trees.

The many new plants that developed attracted different plant-eating dinosaurs.

The small crocodile called *Bernissartia* thrived during the early Cretaceous period.

Animal life

Modern **reptiles** such as snakes appeared in the Cretaceous period. So did small **mammals**. As the land broke up, the dinosaurs began to develop in different ways. They became more diverse as they adapted to new **environments**.

BONEHEADS

The pachycephalosaurs, or boneheads, were a small family of plant-eating dinosaurs that lived in the Cretaceous period. They probably evolved in Asia, but later spread to North America. Boneheads moved on their two back legs and could run quickly if they were threatened by a **predator**.

Living together

Boneheaded dinosaurs probably lived together in **herds**. Males may have used their bony heads to butt each other's flanks at mating time. The animal that won these fights would mate with the females.

DINO DATA

*The dinosaur with the longest name is a bonehead—*Micropachycephalosaurus *(my-kro-pak-ee-KEF-a-loh-SAWR-us).*

Prenocephale did not have a dome, but rather a flat head scattered with bony knobs.

Lumpy heads

Pachycephalosaur means "thick-headed lizard." These strange-looking dinosaurs had high foreheads and dome-shaped lumps on their skulls. These were made of large pieces of thick bone. Some pachycephalosaurs also had bony frills and knobs on their heads.

Stegoceras had one of the thickest skulls of all the pachycephalosaurs.

Head protection

A previously unknown pachycephalosaur, named *Texacephale*, was discovered in 2010. Its dome had a ridge on either side. Some scientists think that these may have acted as shock absorbers to protect the skull during head-butting.

The biggest bonehead

Pachycephalosaurus was the largest of the pachycephalosaurs. Its skull alone was 2 feet (0.6 meter) long. The huge dome on its head was 10 inches (25 centimeters) thick and made of solid bone. It was ringed by lots of smaller bony lumps.

DUCK-BILLED DINOSAURS

The duck-billed dinosaurs are called this because they had long, flat beaks like a duck. Their proper name is hadrosaurs, which simply means "big lizard."

Tsintaosaurus's horn may have been brightly colored.

Long horn

Tsintaosaurus had an unusual horn on its head. The front of the horn may have been covered with a flap of skin that stretched to its snout. The skin could have been blown up like a balloon and used to make signals to other dinosaurs.

Shantungosaurus lived in China in the late Cretaceous period.

Flat head

Shantungosaurus was one of the largest hadrosaurs. It had a flat head and an extra-long, flat tail. Its tail made up nearly half its total body length. *Shantungosaurus* used it to keep its heavy body balanced when walking.

Different duckbills

Hadrosaurs could be found across most of the northern world in Cretaceous times. They were one of the last types of dinosaur to evolve. Hadrosaurs all had a broad, flat snout, but they had different head features. Some, like *Hypacrosaurus*, had large **crests** on their heads.

ARMORED NODOSAURS

Nodosaurs were huge plant-eating beasts. They were closely related to stegosaurs, another group of armoured dinosaurs that began to die out before the Cretaceous. Stegosaurs had club-like tails but nodosaurs had long, tapering tails.

Sauropelta was one of the largest nodosaurs, growing to more than 20 feet (6 meters) long.

The plates on a *Nodosaurus* were covered in thick, leathery skin and horn.

Well-protected

The nodosaurs were heavy, four-legged plant-eaters. They had long, narrow skulls. Long spikes stuck out from their sides and bony plates covered their bodies. If meat-eaters wanted to kill a nodosaur, their main hope was to slash at its soft underside.

DINO DATA

Nodosaurs could pull in their front legs and lie close to the ground to protect themselves against predators.

Panoplosaurus's body armor was made up of broad, square plates arranged in wide bands across its back.

A new nodosaur

In 2011, a new type of nodosaur received its name. Its fossilized remains were discovered in 1997. At less than 1 foot (0.3 meter) long, it was tiny. This was a baby nodosaur that had only just hatched. It was called *Propanoplosaurus*.

CLUB-TAILED DINOSAURS

The ankylosaurs were a lot like their relatives, the nodosaurs. They were all stocky plant-eaters. Like the nodosaur, it was heavily armored, but the ankylosaur had an extra weapon, a large "club" on the end of its tail. Fossils of these well-protected animals have been found on every continent except Africa.

Ankylosaurus was one of the largest in its group, weighing over 5 tons (4.5 tonnes).

Ankylosaur *features*

The ankylosaurs were built like tanks, and some were about the same size! They had huge hips and strong legs to support their heavy bodies. The bony plates on their back and head were thick and strong.

Male ankylosaurs may have used their club tails to fight each other to become leader of their herd.

Club tails

At the tip of an ankylosaur's tail was a large ball of bone. If an ankylosaur was attacked by a meat-eating dinosaur, it would swing its tail from side to side like a club. The heavy ball could seriously hurt or even kill a predator.

Saichania probably fed on tough desert plants in its hot home in Asia.

DINO DATA

The ankylosaur Euoplocephalus *was so well-protected that it even had armored eyelids!*

BIRD MIMICS

This group of dinosaurs is known as the ornithomimids – a name that means "bird mimics". With two long legs and stocky bodies covered in feathers, they looked like some modern birds, such as ostriches and emus. The largest was *Deinochierus*, which grew to 36 feet (11 meters) long and 12 feet (3.6 meters) high.

Pelecanimimus could have held its food in its throat pouch, as a pelican does today.

Ornithomimid variety

The early "pelican-mimic" ornithomimid *Pelecanimimus* was about the size of a turkey. Unlike its later relatives, it had many tiny teeth in its jaws. It also had a pouch beneath its throat like a pelican. It probably waded in shallow water and hunted fish.

A typical ornithomimid

The most typical ornithomimid was *Struthiomimus*. The name means "ostrich mimic" and indeed it was about the size of an ostrich, with long ostrich legs, and a long ostrichlike neck. It also had a toothless beak and it probably ate mostly plants, which it could grab with its long, three-fingered hands.

DINO DATA

With their long, powerful legs, bird mimics were the fastest group of dinosaurs.

MOSASAURS

While dinosaurs roamed on land, there were monstrous beasts in the sea. Mososaurs were the deadliest predators in the oceans. There were about 70 different types of mososaur, and these giant sea lizards swam in waters all over the world.

Mosasaur jaws were lined with strong teeth to bite and crush **prey.**

An exciting discovery

The first mosasaur was found more than 200 years ago. Some giant jaw bones were discovered in Holland. At first, experts thought they belonged to a whale. When they later realized that the bones were from a huge lizard, they called it a *Mosasaurus*—or "lizard from the Meuse river."

DINO DATA

Despite their size, mosasaurs were not always safe from attack. A mosasaur fossil has been found with a shark bite on its spine.

Mosasaur movement

Mosasaurs may have been quite fast swimmers. They moved their long tails from side to side to power themselves through the water. Their **flippers** were used for steering. Mosasaurs glided along the bottom of the sea, looking for prey.

The mosasaur *Tylosaurus* used its snout to locate food.

The biggest beast

The largest mosasaur ever discovered is *Mosasaurus hoffmanni*. This huge beast was 50 feet (15 meters) long. Its usual food would have been fish and squid, but it also attacked ammonites. Many ammonite shells have been found with mosasaur teeth-marks on them!

PTERANODON

No dinosaurs could fly, but there were plenty of flying reptiles in Cretaceous skies. *Pteranodon* had a short tail, huge wings, and fur-like fluff on its skin to keep it warm.

DINO DATA

Pteranodon *had a big brain in its large head and was probably quite intelligent.*

Moving on land

Scientists have found fossil footprints of pterosaurs such as *Pteranodon* close to dinosaur footprints. The footprints suggest that pterosaurs may have walked on four legs when they were on land.

Toothless feeding

Unlike many other pterosaurs, *Pteranodon* did not have any teeth. Like pelicans, it fed by scooping up fish in its jaws and then swallowing them whole.

Pteranodon had a wingspan of about 23 feet (7 meters).

Take-off and flight

As a fish-eater, *Pteranodon* probably lived near water. Fossils have been found close to seas and oceans. It may have launched itself into the air from the edge of cliffs. *Pteranodon* was a skillful flyer and could travel a long way gliding on its huge wings.

Head crest

Pteranodon had a large crest on the top of its head. This may have balanced or steered its short, heavy body in the air. The bright colors of the crest might also have been used to attract mates.

MICRORAPTOR

These little dinosaurs could not fly like birds do today. They did not have the muscles for it. However, they were able to glide from tree to tree like modern flying squirrels.

Microraptor was about the size of a pigeon. It had flight feathers on its arms and legs, giving it four wings.

Theropods

Microraptors belonged to a group of dinosaurs called theropods. Theropods walked on two legs and most of them hunted other animals to eat.

Searching for food

The four-winged theropods—*Microraptor* and its relatives—hunted for insects and little tree animals in the branches of the forests. They could have swooped down out of the sky, catching their prey by surprise. Their long claws enabled them to cling to vertical tree trunks.

Furry for warmth

The covering of tiny feathers seen in *Sinosauropteryx* and other small theropods would not have developed for flight. The feathers would have evolved as insulation to keep the body at a constant temperature while they ran about, just like mammals and birds do today. Gliding and flying feathers developed from this fine covering.

The feathers of *Sinosauropteryx* were no more than an overall covering of fine **down**.

Changyuraptor was very similar to *Microraptor*, but much bigger—about the size of a turkey.

DINO DATA

Although gliding dinosaurs have only been found in China so far, they probably lived in all the forests of the early Cretaceous world.

VELOCIRAPTOR

Velociraptor belonged to the dinosaur group dromaeosaurs, or raptors. It lived in the hot, dry regions of Asia 85 million years ago. Its name means "speedy thief."

Small but deadly

Velociraptor has a reputation as a large and terrifying killer. In fact, like most other dromaeosaurs, it was only about the size of a big chicken! *Velociraptor* was a fierce hunter. This meat-eater had a long, upturned snout containing 80 sharp, curved teeth. It also had viciously sharp claws.

We know that *Velociraptor* was feathered because well-preserved fossils, with clearly visible feathers, of its smaller relative *Sinornithosaurus* were found in China.

Fight to the death

In Mongolia, scientists found the skeletons of two dinosaurs. They had died while fighting each other. The *Velociraptor* was gripping the *Protoceratops*' head in its hands. Its clawed feet were ripping into the horned dinosaur's belly. The *Protoceratops* had crushed the *Velociraptor's* chest.

DINO DATA

Velociraptor *may have pinned down its victim and started eating it while it was still alive.*

TRICERATOPS

Great herds of horned *Triceratops* lived in western North America. They survived to the end of the Cretaceous period, 66 million years ago. *Triceratops* means "three-horned face."

DINO DATA

Triceratops *lived at the same time and in the same places as* Tyrannosaurus, *so it was probably hunted by that terrifying meat-eater.*

Great weight

Triceratops was the largest and heaviest horned dinosaur. It could weigh up to 11 tons (10 tonnes). Its skull alone was more than 6.5 feet (2 meters) long. It had strong legs to support its weight.

Triceratops's frill may have been to protect its neck from the jaws of predators, or as a mating display.

Horned dinosaurs

Ceratopsians, or horned dinosaurs, had beak-like mouths and long, pointed horns. A sheet of bone, called a frill, grew from the back of the skull.

Feeding habits

Although it looked dangerous, *Triceratops* was a **herbivore**. It fed on plants and grasses that grew close to the ground. Its horny beak helped it tear the plants. Strong cheek teeth ground them up in its mouth.

TYRANNOSAURUS

One of the most famous dinosaurs, *Tyrannosaurus*, was a powerful **prehistoric** killer. At about 13 feet (4 meters) tall and weighing 8 tons (7 tonnes), this was one of the mightiest meat-eaters ever to walk on Earth.

Tyrannosaurus had thick, strong teeth at the front for holding on to prey.

Big body, small arms

Like other theropods, *Tyrannosaurus* walked upright. Its back legs were large and strong. In contrast, its arms were too tiny to even reach its own mouth! The sharp claws on its hands were deadly weapons.

Ambush attacker

Tyrannosaurus would **ambush** its prey. It hid in the trees, then sneaked up on grazing plant-eaters. In a short burst of speed, it would rush out and grab its victim in its massive, powerful jaws. Although it was a big animal, *Tyrannosaurus* did not need to kill every day. A feast of a large plant-eating dinosaur could keep *Tyrannosaurus* going for several weeks.

Some scientists think that *Tyrannosaurus* may have **scavenged** for food.

DINO DATA

Tyrannosaurus's *massive head could be more than 4 feet (1.2 meters) long.*

Tyrannosaurus died out along with many other animals at the end of the Cretaceous period.

THE END OF AN ERA

The meteorite would have exploded with the force of thousands of atomic bombs.

The Cretaceous ended 66 million years ago, when a catastrophic event changed the world forever. At least 80 percent of all types of animals and plants died out, including the dinosaurs.

Meteorite impact

The remains of a huge **meteorite** crater have been found in Mexico. Scientists believe that when the meteorite crashed into Earth, it caused a massive explosion, setting off volcanic eruptions, floods, and earthquakes. Clouds of **toxic** dust and gases filled the skies and blocked out the Sun.

Without sunlight, most plants died and plant-eating animals starved. Eventually, the meat-eaters that fed on them died out too.

DINO DATA

It may have taken up to 200,000 years for the pterosaurs, sea reptiles, and many dinosaurs to die out completely.

Survivors

Scientists continue to make exciting discoveries that allow them to piece together the amazing story of life on Earth. We now know that long before the meteorite hit Earth, some dinosaurs had evolved into a group of animals we call "birds." Like many mammals, non-dinosaur reptiles, and amphibians, some birds survived the meteorite impact.

As the Sun was blocked out, plants and animals slowly died out.

PICTURE CREDITS

Key: FC = front cover, BC = back cover, t = top, b = bottom, c = center, r = right, l = left.

Alamy:
10/11 Stocktrek Images Inc; 14-15 Stocktrek Images Inc.

All Canada Photos:
18-19 vario images GmbH & Co.KG.

Beehive Illustration:
6-7 Mark Turner.

Dreamstime:
5tr Mr1805; 18br Mr1805.

Getty Images:
1 De Agostini; 4/5 Mark Stevenson/Corbis/Stocktrek Images; 8tr Kevin Schafer/Corbis, 9 De Agostini; 14c Nobumichi Tamura/Stocktrek Images, 15tl Sergey Krasovskiy; 17cr DEA Picture Library; 20cr Corey Ford, 20-21 Sergey Krasovskiy, 21tl Dorling Kindersley; 24-25 Louie Psihoyos/Corbis; 28tr Sanford/Anglioto/Corbis.

Natural History Museum:
22br Geological Museum of China.

Shutterstock:
FC Orla; BC Daniel Eskridge; 7tl Michael Rosskothen; 12-13 yanikap; 16-17 Rich Carey; 24br haraldmuc; 26bl Konstyantyn Ivanyshen, 26-27 DM7; 30 haraldmuc.

GLOSSARY

ambush
launch a surprise attack on another animal

continent
a very large area of land surrounded by ocean

crest
a raised area or ridge on top of the head; some animals have crests of colorful feathers

down
soft, fluffy feathers that trap air and help to keep an animal warm

environment
the natural surroundings where an animal or plant lives

Equator
an imaginary line around the middle of the Earth, separating it into two halves called hemispheres

flipper
a paddle-like limb that is used to swim

fossil
the remains of a long-dead animal or plant that have, over time, been turned into stone

herbivore
an animal that eats plants

herd
a group of animals that feeds on grass and other plants

mammal
an animal that has hair or fur and feeds its young with milk. Most mammals give birth to their young; just a few species lay eggs

meteorite
rock or metal that falls to the Earth's surface from outer space; when the object is flying through space, it is called a meteor

predator
an animal that hunts other animals to eat

prehistoric
describes a time long before humans lived on Earth, or could write about their world

prey
an animal that is hunted by other animals for food

reptile
a scaly-skinned animal; most reptiles lay their eggs on land, although some reptiles give birth instead

scavenge
eat the remains of dead animals or plants

toxic
poisonous

INDEX